SCREAM STREET

Book Eight

ATTACK OF THE TROLLS

The fiendish fun continues at

www.screamstreet.com

SCREAM STREET

Book Eight
ATTACK OF THE TROLLS

TOMMY DNBAVAND

CANDLEWICK PRESS

Text copyright © 2010 by Tommy Donbavand
Illustrations copyright © 2010 by Cartoon Saloon Ltd.

First U.S. edition 2012

Library of Congress Cataloging-in-Publication Data is available.

Library of Congress Catalog Card Number pending

ISBN 978-0-7636-5760-4

12 13 14 15 16 17 18 QGB 10 9 8 7 6 5 4 3 2 1

Printed in Burlington, WI, U.S.A.

This book was typeset in Bembo Educational.
The illustrations were done in ink.

Candlewick Press
99 Dover Street
Somerville, Massachusetts 02144

visit us at www.candlewick.com

For Luke Donbavand,
the star behind Scream Street

Meet the residents

Luke Watson

Cleo Farr

Resus Negative

Dixon

Sir Otto Sneer

Samuel Skipstone

Alston and Bella Negative

Eefa Everwell

Doug

Dr. Skully

Niles Farr

Mr. and Mrs. Watson

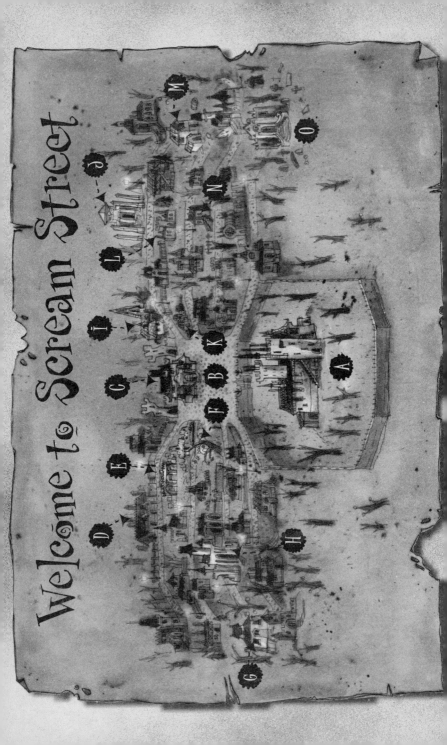

Who lives where

A Sneer Hall

B Central Square

C Everwell's Emporium

D No. 2: The Crudleys

E No. 5: The Movers

F No. 11: Twinkle

G No. 13: Luke Watson

H No. 14: Resus Negative

I No. 21: Eefa Everwell

J No. 22: Cleo Farr

K No. 26: The Headless Horseman

L No. 27: Femur Ribs

M No. 28: Doug, Turf, and Berry

N No. 32: Simon Howl

O No. 39: The Skullys

Previously on Scream Street...

Mr. and Mrs. Watson were terrified when their son, Luke, first transformed into a werewolf. But that was nothing compared to their terror at being forcibly moved to Scream Street— and discovering that there was no going back.

Determined to take his parents home, Luke enlisted the help of his new friends, Resus Negative, a wannabe vampire, and Cleo Farr, an Egyptian mummy, to find six relics left behind by the community's founding fathers. Only by collecting these magical artifacts would he be able to open a doorway back to his own world.

Just as Luke and his friends finally succeeded in their quest, Mr. and Mrs. Watson realized how happy Luke had become in his new home and decided to stay on in Scream Street. But the newly opened doorway was becoming a problem—Sir Otto Sneer, the street's wicked landlord, was charging "normals" from Luke's world to visit what he called "the world's greatest freak show."

To protect Scream Street, Luke, Resus, and Cleo must try to close the doorway by returning the relics to their original owners—beginning with the fang of an ancient vampire. . . .

Chapter One
The Coffin

Three ghostly black figures scurried silently across Scream Street's central square as the moon glimmered behind a scattering of thin clouds. Inside a nearby house, a clock chimed midnight.

Keeping to the shadows as much as possible, the figures crept past a thin, red-haired man sitting beside a doorway of shimmering light. The

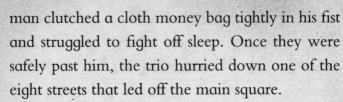

man clutched a cloth money bag tightly in his fist and struggled to fight off sleep. Once they were safely past him, the trio hurried down one of the eight streets that led off the main square.

As they approached a large house halfway along the street, one of the figures removed a black glove. Then he slipped a long fingernail into the crack above a first-floor window and slid his hand from left to right. The lock clicked, and the window was raised.

The figures climbed inside, and another of them pulled off a balaclava and gasped for air. "I can't breathe in that thing!" hissed Cleo Farr.

"How can you say that?" whispered Resus Negative, appearing from under his own balaclava and quickly pulling in his vampire's cape before it got trapped in the closing window. "You're a mummy. You're wrapped from head to toe in bandages!"

"Yes," retorted Cleo, "but my bandages don't cover my nose and mouth!"

The third figure, Luke Watson, tore off his own head covering. "Will you two keep quiet?" he snapped. "We need to do this without waking anyone, remember?"

"I still don't see why we can't wait until morning and simply ask permission to go down to the Crudleys' cellar," admitted Resus. "They let us last time."

"We've been through this," said Luke. "The fewer people who know what we're planning to do, the better." He pulled a long vampire's fang from his pocket and held it up to the shaft of moonlight that streamed through the window.

Resus sighed. "We really have to give it back?" The fang had belonged to one of his ancestors, Count Negatov, and was one of six relics the trio had collected in order to open a doorway out of Scream Street so Luke could take his parents back to their own world.

Luke nodded. "Yep—and as soon as possible. Come on. . . ." He led the way along the dark hallway toward the bog monsters' living room.

After the three friends had finally opened the magical doorway out of Scream Street, Luke's parents had decided to stay in their new home — much to the delight of their son and his friends.

The doorway, however, had remained open, and Scream Street's landlord, Sir Otto Sneer, had begun charging people from Luke's world

3

to visit "the world's greatest freak show." These normals were gradually making life unbearable for the community's unusual residents, and Luke and his friends had tried desperately to discover how to close the doorway once and for all. Now they thought they might have figured it out: they just needed to return all the relics to their respective founding fathers, thus reversing the magic. Or so they hoped.

"Do you really think that if Mr. and Mrs. Crudley found out, they'd tell Sir Otto we were giving back the relics?" asked Cleo as they entered the dimly lit living room.

"I'd like to think not," replied Luke, "but we can't be sure. And Sneer won't be happy once he discovers we're trying to close the doorway, so the longer—"

Snorble!

All three children froze. It sounded like someone blowing bubbles in a vat of lumpy pudding.

"What," said Cleo, "was *that*?"

"There!" whispered Luke. Resus and Cleo followed his pointing finger. Lying back in a vast, plush armchair was the massive, gooey bulk of Mr. Crudley—one of Scream Street's bog

 4

monsters. A book entitled *Great Expectorations* lay open on his slime-coated stomach.

Snorble!

"He's asleep!" said Cleo, relieved. "At least, I *think* that's snoring. . . ."

"Let's just get to the cellar," hissed Luke, beginning to creep as silently as he could across the thick carpet. The Crudleys were incredibly

house-proud, and a large amount of designer furniture littered the overdecorated room. "We just have to be careful that we don't—OW!" Luke yelled as he cracked his shin on a marble coffee table.

"Wha'? Wassat?" gurgled Mr. Crudley, jolting awake. Luke, Resus, and Cleo hurled themselves behind the chair just as two eyes appeared near the top of the hideous mound of gloop. Mr. Crudley yawned widely, picked up his book, and began to read.

"What do we do now?" mouthed Resus. Luke shrugged.

Cleo gestured for her friends to be silent, then in a soft, gentle voice, she began to sing: *"Hush, Mr. Crudley, don't say a word, Daddy's gonna buy you a mockingbird. . . ."*

"What are you doing?" whispered Resus. "He'll hear you, and—"

He stopped as Mr. Crudley yawned again and allowed his eyes to droop.

"He's dropping off," Luke whispered back. "Keep going!"

"And if that mockingbird don't sing, Daddy's gonna buy you a diamond ring," Cleo continued, her voice

low and soothing. The bog monster grunted and began to breathe more deeply.

Resus signaled that he wanted to take over. *"And if that diamond ring won't do, Daddy's gonna buy you . . . a pile of poo!"*

Snorb—"Wha'?" Mr. Crudley sat bolt upright, and Resus clamped his hand over his mouth to try to stifle his giggles. Luke shot him a look, then waved to Cleo to take over again.

"And if that, er . . . pile of poo smells gross, Daddy's gonna buy you a billy goat." Mr. Crudley settled back in his chair and closed his eyes again. *"And if that billy goat's too tough—"*

"Daddy's gonna let off a rasping guff," interjected Resus.

"Quiet!" hissed Cleo, a little too loudly. Mr. Crudley turned in his chair, the book sinking into the folds of his stomach, and gurgled. The children held their breath, until . . . *Snorble!*

The trio crept out from their hiding place, and Luke punched Resus in the arm. "You idiot," he scolded. "You could have got us all caught!"

"Funny, though, wasn't it?" Resus grinned.

Luke crossed the room and opened the door to the Crudleys' cellar. In their basement was a

manhole that led directly to the sewers—and the resting place of Count Negatov.

When the door was safely closed behind them, Resus pulled a flaming torch from his cloak and illuminated the way down the steep wooden stairs. The trio quickly located the manhole and, with a little effort, slid the cover to one side.

"Who's going first?" asked Cleo.

"I think it should be Resus for nearly waking Mr. Crudley," said Luke, nudging the vampire with his elbow.

"All right," groaned Resus, handing Luke the torch. "I'll be the brave one!" He found the rungs of a ladder with his feet and climbed down into the darkness of the tunnel below.

Cleo followed, and then Luke. "We need to head farther into the sewers, don't we?" he asked.

"Yep," said Resus, taking the torch again. "That way . . ."

The trio walked deeper and deeper into the damp sewers until eventually they came to a large underground cavern, its walls coated with glowing green gutweed.

As they no longer needed its light, Resus

pushed the torch back into his cloak. "Last time we were down here, there were thousands of goblins waiting for us."

Cleo shuddered at the memory. "I can't hear them now," she said.

"No one's seen a goblin in Scream Street for weeks," Luke assured her. "Mr. Skipstone thinks they've found a new home in another G.H.O.U.L. community."

"Well I'm glad we won't have to fight our way to the coffin this time," said Resus, heading over to a stone casket that stood in the center of the cavern. "Hey, wait a minute. The lid's not on properly!"

"Then it won't be as hard to open as it was last time," said Luke. "Come on."

The trio pressed their hands against the lid and pushed, sliding it off the stone coffin. They waved dust from the air as it crashed to the ground.

"Count Negatov," declared Luke, taking the fang from his pocket a second time. "You honored me with your gift as founding father, but now I must return it to you for—"

"Keep going, my dear—*hic!*" announced a voice. "Your words are very—*hic*—soothing!"

Luke stared down at where he had expected to see the ancient vampire. Instead, grinning up at him from the coffin, was a zombie.

Chapter Two
The Meeting

Luke yawned as he set off for school the next morning. It had been a long night.

After finding Berry, one of Scream Street's three resident zombies, lying in the coffin instead of Count Negatov, the trio had set about escorting her home. From her slurred explanation, they gathered she had been playing hide-and-seek with her undead friends. In her intoxicated state, however, the creature had insisted on dancing with each of the children in turn before they left the sewers. By the time Luke's head hit the pillow, his sneakers were coated in mud and he had almost mastered the foxtrot.

Resus and Cleo were now waiting for him in the central square, which was already filled with tourists. The normals were exploring the gardens, shooting footage of the oddly shaped houses and trying to persuade the residents to have their pictures taken alongside them.

Sitting by the shimmering, rainbow-colored doorway to Luke's world was Scream Street's landlord, Sir Otto Sneer. He glared at the trio as they passed, then returned to stuffing fistfuls of cash into his pockets as more normals streamed through the arch.

"Come in and see the freaks!" he bellowed, then sucked on a noxious cigar. "Horrible, stinking vampires, mummies, and werewolves—right here!"

"*He's* the horrible one," grumbled Cleo under her breath. "Scream Street is *our* home, and we

should be able to come and go without people gawking at us."

Luke sighed as he remembered the day the normals had arrived. At first the residents had tried to hide their unusual qualities with disguises and makeup and had made sure that their more bizarre-looking neighbors stayed indoors. The deception had looked like it might work—until Luke's mom had unexpectedly transformed into a werewolf, confirming for the visitors once and for all the true nature of the street's inhabitants. Now everyone simply tried to ignore the tourists and get on with their lives as best they could, although it was proving increasingly difficult.

"I hate this!" snapped Resus. "How would Sneer like it if he had normals trampling all over his—"

The vampire stopped mid-sentence as he was suddenly jerked backward.

"Give me a turn with your cape!"

Resus spun around to find a teenage boy pulling hard on his cape. The boy's friend swigged from a can of Coke and laughed at his friend's antics.

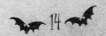 14

"Let go," Resus warned.

The teenager stepped up to him and glared. "Or what?" he growled. "You gonna bite my neck and drink my blood?"

"For your information," Cleo announced haughtily, "vampires in Scream Street don't bite people. Their kitchen sinks have three faucets and—"

"Cleo!" hissed Resus. "This isn't exactly the time."

The teenager wrapped the end of the cape around his wrist and pulled harder. "What's the matter, fang-face?" he snorted. "Need your girlfriend to stick up for you?"

"She is *not* my girlfriend," declared Resus.

"I'm not surprised!" exclaimed the second boy, draining the last of his drink and tossing the can over a nearby hedge. "Who'd go out with someone as ugly as that? She looks like she's been in an accident!"

"Let go of the cape and walk away *now*!" Luke commanded angrily.

The two boys shared a glance, then burst out laughing. "How about you *make* us, shorty?"

 15

Luke was beginning to feel the first stage of his werewolf transformation coming on. "Keep talking and I might just do that," he warned.

Cleo grabbed his arm. "Luke, don't!" she hissed. "You could really hurt them."

"Him?" The boy still clutching Resus's cape laughed. "The only thing he could possibly hurt is my knuckles!" He clenched his other fist and pulled his arm back.

Luke felt his bones begin to crack and reshape, but his transformation wasn't happening quickly enough. The teenager was likely to break his jaw before his fur had even begun to sprout.

The boy grinned and swung his fist toward Luke — only to have it stopped in midair by a larger hand. A larger, green-skinned hand covered in scabs and weeping sores.

"Dudes!" cried a voice. "This isn't in the spirit of peace and harmony!"

The teenager spun around to find himself face-to-face with Doug, one of Scream Street's zombies. Insects crawled through the creature's greasy, matted hair, and stinking pus oozed from cracks in his rotting skin.

"You kids should learn to play nice," said

Doug with a smile, revealing a family of cock-roaches scuttling around his few remaining teeth.

The teenager screamed and finally released his grip on Resus's cape. Then he ran away across the square, his friend struggling to keep up.

"Hey, where are those two dudes going?" asked Doug, producing the empty Coke can. "I was going to ask if they had any more of this stuff. The roaches dig it, man!" He stuck out his diseased tongue and allowed the last few drops of fizzy drink to splash onto it. The cockroaches clicked happily and began to drink.

"Thanks for your help, Doug," said Luke

as the anger began to ebb away. His werewolf transformation had only got as far as a few reshaped bones, and they were already returning to normal.

"No problemo, little dude," Doug said. "You guys were there for Berry last night when she fell asleep in that coffin." He rubbed his forehead, peeling away a large flap of skin as he did so. "Man, that fermented spinal fluid really went to my head. I totally forgot to go look for her and Turf! It's good to know you cats were on the case."

"Our pleasure," said Resus. "Although we weren't actually looking for Berry. We were hoping to find—" Luke threw his friend a warning look. ". . . someone else," the vampire quickly finished. "But we can't say who," he added.

The zombie tapped the side of his nose. "It's OK, dudes—I'm up to speed on the secrecy deal. In fact, the head honcho himself sent me out here to track you down. He wants to rap with you in private."

"Who is it?" asked Luke. "Who wants to talk to us?"

A figure stepped out of the shadows at the edge of the square. "I do."

"I hear you've worked out how to close the doorway to the normals' world," said Zeal Chillchase, unlocking the door to one of the few empty houses in Scream Street and quickly ushering the trio inside.

"Who told you that?" asked Luke, amazed. "I haven't discussed it with anyone, except . . ." He turned to Resus and Cleo. "I told you not to talk about it!"

"Don't look at us," snapped Cleo. "We haven't said a word!"

"I am the most successful Tracker G.H.O.U.L. has ever employed," interjected Chillchase. "There is very little I don't know. Now, tell me what you plan to do."

Luke flopped down onto a dusty sofa. He'd wanted to keep his idea between himself and his friends, but he should have known that Zeal Chillchase would find out about it. The Tracker's job was to locate unusual life-forms and arrange for them to be rehoused by the Government Housing of Unusual Life-forms; he was the one who'd found Luke and relocated him and his

family to Scream Street. Zeal was bound to discover sooner or later what Luke had in mind.

"We have to give the relics we collected back to the founding fathers," said Luke.

"And you think this will cause the doorway to close?" asked Chillchase. "What evidence do you have that it will work?"

"None," admitted Luke. "It's just a hunch, really."

"A *hunch*?"

Luke went red. "I know it sounds crazy," he said defensively. "I just have a feeling that giving back the fang might cause the doorway to close — or at least begin to disappear. Maybe one of the colors will vanish or something. . . ."

"But there are *six* colors in the doorway," the Tracker reminded him.

"And six relics to give back!" Cleo said. "Once we've returned all of them, the idea is that the doorway will close permanently."

Zeal mulled over the idea for a moment. "OK," he said eventually. "I agree — you should return the relics and see what happens."

"We tried to make a start last night," said Resus. "It just didn't work out."

 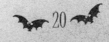

"What do you mean?"

"We went down into the sewers to visit Count Negatov's coffin," explained Luke. "But he wasn't in it."

"He wouldn't have been," said Chillchase. "His body was returned to his ancestral castle several weeks ago."

"In that case, we're stuck," said Cleo. "There's no way we can give his fang back now."

"Ah, but there is," said Chillchase with a smile. "If I send you there."

Chapter Three
The Transformation

The Hex Hatch opened like a window in the air. Through it, Luke, Resus, and Cleo could see a harsh, rugged landscape. Endless fields cowered beneath a heavy sky, and the summit of a distant mountain was swallowed by bleak gray clouds.

"Count Negatov's castle is at the top of that peak," explained Zeal Chillchase.

Resus stared at the Tracker. "You think we should go *now*?" he asked.

"I see no reason to delay your departure."

"What about school?" asked Cleo. "Dr. Skully won't be happy if we simply don't show up."

"The quest might take some time," replied Chillchase. "I will speak to your teacher. Lessons can be canceled for the time being."

Resus grinned.

"Although once the doorway is closed, you'll be expected to catch up on the work you have missed."

Resus scowled.

"It shouldn't take you more than twenty-four hours to get to the castle and back," said the Tracker.

"I can't be away that long!" cried Resus. "It's Vampire New Year tonight."

Luke raised an eyebrow. "Vampire New Year?" he scoffed. "You're making that up!"

"I am not," retorted Resus. "Look—I've got

a load of party food and fireworks ready!" He pulled a handful of cupcakes and sparklers from his cloak.

"There's our parents as well," added Cleo. "They'll notice if we disappear."

"I shall ensure that your parents approve of your quest," promised Zeal.

"I'm really starting to dislike this idea," grumbled Resus as he pushed the party supplies back into his cape.

"Why is G.H.O.U.L. helping us?" Luke asked cautiously.

"G.H.O.U.L. is *not* helping you," replied Zeal Chillchase. "I'm acting in a purely unofficial capacity. In fact, should anything happen to you, I shall have to deny all knowledge of your expedition."

"Wow," quipped Resus. "Way to sell it!"

"OK," said Luke. "So why are *you* helping us?"

Chillchase sighed. "I've let matters get out of control," he admitted. "Moving a werewolf to Scream Street should have been a simple procedure, yet you and your friends have proved . . . shall we say, difficult to control. If G.H.O.U.L.

was to discover I'd allowed a doorway to be opened between Luke's world and Scream Street, I would be stripped of my position."

Cleo gasped. "We don't want you to lose your job!" she exclaimed.

"But I like the idea of being difficult to control," said Resus with a grin.

Zeal glared down at him but carried on. "However, if your theory is correct, the door should close once all the relics are returned," he growled. "So, the sooner you begin, the better. And that means going through this Hex Hatch."

"Where exactly *is* that?" asked Luke, staring through the magical window at the coarse grass and clumps of blackened weeds.

"It is a G.H.O.U.L. community in a remote area of what used to be called Transylvania," explained Chillchase. "Aside from the castle, it's now mostly abandoned."

"If it's abandoned, why can't you get us any closer?" asked Resus. "You said the castle's at the top of that mountain—that's miles away!"

"G.H.O.U.L. would instantly spot a Hex Hatch opening so close to the resting place of a founding father," said Zeal. "This is as close as I can get you, I'm afraid." He frowned down at the children through his mirrored sunglasses. "Now go to your parents. You leave in one hour."

Luke arrived home to discover a crowd of people outside his front gate. Among them was Sir Otto Sneer's nephew, Dixon.

"And this is the house where two of Scream Street's most ferocious residents live," he was saying. "Luke Watson and his mother are both killer werewolves. . . ."

A man in a bright pink shirt began to take photographs of the house. "Will we be able to see them attack someone?" he asked eagerly.

Luke pushed his way to the front of the group. "What are you doing, Dixon?"

Sir Otto's nephew squealed at the sight of him and tumbled to the ground. "Ow! I bumped my head!" he whined.

"Stop moaning—you'll be fine," grunted Luke, helping him to his feet. "Now tell me, what are you doing here with all these people?"

"It was Uncle Otto's idea," said Dixon, his bottom lip quivering. "He said the normals have just been wandering around, looking for the freaks—I mean, er . . . for something to see. He said they'd pay good money to be shown who lives where." A look of horror flickered across his face. "Don't tell him I told you!" he wailed.

"I won't," said Luke shortly. "Just take these people—"

Suddenly, the front door opened and Mrs. Watson marched out. "What's going on?" she demanded. "What are you all doing here?"

"Mom, it's OK . . ." began Luke, hurrying up the path.

"He called her 'Mom'!" said the man in the pink shirt excitedly. "That must be them. The mother and son killer werewolves!"

The yard lit up as dozens of cameras began to flash.

"Get out of here—now!" yelled Mrs. Watson.

"Mom, you *have* to calm down," urged Luke. "You can't let them upset you."

"I'm already upset!" countered his mom. "Why can't they just leave us alone?"

"Show us your fangs!" a young woman called from the crowd.

"Can I record a howl for my ring tone?" bellowed a man in a suit, holding up his cell phone.

"Come on," said Luke, grabbing his mom by the hand. "Let's get inside."

As Mrs. Watson turned to go back into the house, she cracked her elbow against the doorframe and let out a cry of pain. She had broken her arm on her first day in Scream Street, and it was still tender.

"Sorry," said the man in the suit. "I wasn't recording—could you do that again?"

28

"Get them away from here, Dixon!" snapped Luke as he pulled his mom into the house and slammed the door shut. The silence of the hallway closed over them.

"You can't let it bother you," said Luke, turning to his mom. "It'll just make you—"

He froze. Mrs. Watson was gripping her injured arm, her face twisted in pain . . . her werewolf transformation was beginning.

"Just breathe slowly," instructed Luke, and he led her over to sit on the stairs. "The anger's already inside you, but you can't let it take control."

"Am I . . . ? Am I going to turn into that . . . that *thing* again?" asked his mom through gritted teeth. It was less than a week since she had experienced her first transformation, and the idea of becoming a werewolf again terrified her.

"Not if I can help it," said Luke firmly. "At least, not all of you." Since arriving in Scream Street, Luke had discovered the ability to focus his transformation on just one area of his body, allowing only that part to change. He hoped his mom would be able to do the same.

"Imagine the anger as a liquid," he told her. "Like black ink flowing through your veins. Now

picture it running down your arm—nowhere else, just down that arm."

Mrs. Watson closed her eyes and whimpered as she fought to control the transformation. Bones cracked in her arm as they stretched and grew, the muscles warping into new shapes. Dark-blond fur burst through the skin and long, yellowing talons sliced through the tips of her fingers.

"That's it, Mom!" cried Luke. "You're doing it!"

Whiskers sprouted on either side of Mrs. Watson's nose, and, for a brief moment, Luke was worried that she would undergo a full transformation and he would be stuck inside the house with an angry werewolf.

"Concentrate!" he said sharply. "Let it all go to your arm."

After a few moments, Mrs. Watson slumped back against the stairs. "How did I do?"

Luke glanced from her werewolf's arm to the whiskers sprouting from her face. "You did great!" He grinned.

"Does this mean I won't ever . . .?" His mom's words faded away.

Luke shook his head. "You'll still become the

wolf from time to time," he explained. "But it gets easier. You'll be able to control the partial transformations more and more."

"What about the visitors?" asked Mrs. Watson, nodding toward the door. "Like the people out there. What happens if I transform near one of them?"

"You just have to hope you don't hurt anyone."

Mrs. Watson was silent for a moment, then she lifted her hand to examine the long, razor-sharp claws. "Still, I guess I'll never have a problem peeling an orange again!" she joked, before bursting into tears.

Luke put his arms around his mom and hugged her tightly.

Chapter Four
The Moors

Luke tapped the crystal ball that he held in his hand. "It doesn't seem to be working yet," he said, peering into its milky-white center.

"Zeal Chillchase said you'd have to be at least a few miles from Scream Street for it to work," Cleo reminded him.

"Yeah," said Resus. "You can still see the Hex Hatch from here."

Luke glanced over his shoulder across the bleak moors behind them. In the distance, he could just make out a hazy window in the air, through which the figure of the Tracker could be seen watching their progress.

Chillchase had lent the three friends a crystal ball that allowed them to look back at life in Scream Street while they were away. This meant they would be able to see whether returning the fang would start to disable the doorway. Luke also wanted to use it to keep an eye on what was happening back home.

"Your mom will be fine," insisted Resus, pulling his foot out of a muddy hole. "Although I can't say the same for my shoes. I don't think they're going to survive this trip."

"Her arm still hadn't changed back when I left," said Luke. "Her werewolf transformations seem to last a lot longer than mine ever do."

"I expect it's nothing to worry about," Cleo reassured him. "It might just be because she started transforming later than you. She was an adult the first time it happened, after all."

"Perhaps," said Luke, unconvinced. He peered into the crystal ball one last time, just in case.

Seeing nothing but hissing static, he shoved it into the pocket of his jacket and continued walking.

Ahead, the landscape was the same as far as the eye could see: miles and miles of rough scrubland. Occasionally small bushes pushed their way out of the tough soil, but there was nothing above waist height apart from the occasional twisted, ink-black skeletons of dead trees.

"Looks like G.H.O.U.L. bought up every rotting tree in existence and had them all shipped to its communities," quipped Cleo.

"How far is this castle?" asked Resus, pulling his cloak free as it snagged on yet another low, spiky shrub. "Are we there yet?"

Cleo struggled not to laugh. "We've been walking for less than half an hour," she said. "Don't tell me you've had enough already."

"Of course not!" retorted Resus. "I just wondered, that's all."

Luke stared out across the miles of empty moorland ahead of them. On the horizon, he could see a densely wooded area where the land rose to eventually become the mountain on which Count Negatov's castle stood. "If we keep going at this pace, we should reach those trees by nightfall," he said thoughtfully.

"Nightfall?" spluttered Resus. "You mean we won't get to the castle today?"

"Probably not," said Cleo.

"But . . . there are no houses or anything!" Resus exclaimed, his eyes sweeping the dark greens and purples of the countryside. "Where are we going to stay?"

"We'll just have to rough it a bit," said Luke. "It'll be fun—like camping. My mom and dad used to take me camping every summer before we came to Scream Street. It's a good time once you get used to the cold and damp."

"Let me get this straight," said Resus. "We're sleeping *outdoors*?"

Luke sighed. "What were you expecting?" he asked. "A cozy little bed-and-breakfast with hot-and-cold-running blood?"

"Of course not!" said Resus. "But I thought there might at least be a farm or a village where we could—"

"Quiet!" hissed Cleo suddenly. "Listen!"

The three kids stopped dead in their tracks

and listened hard. Aside from the wind skimming across the heather, all was silent.

"I can't hear anything," said Resus.

"There," said Cleo, pointing. "It came from there!"

Luke followed her gaze to a dark-green shape sticking up from the ground nearby. "That's just a bush," he said.

"But it made a noise," insisted Cleo.

"What kind of noise?" asked Resus.

"A sort of honking noise," said Cleo, already wishing she hadn't mentioned it.

Resus made a mock-terrified face. "Don't tell me we're being followed by the dreaded Transylvanian honking bush!" he gasped.

Cleo slapped him on the arm. "I thought I heard something," she snapped.

"It's probably just your imagination," said Luke. "This is pretty desolate countryside. It would be easy for your mind to start playing tricks."

"And it doesn't help if you're half crazy to begin with," joked Resus. He leaped backward as Cleo swung a leg in his direction, then there was a squelch as his foot landed in another gooey brown puddle. "Oh, great!"

"Serves you right," said Cleo, sticking her tongue out at him.

Ignoring her, Resus reached into his cloak and pulled out a cloth and brush.

"What are you doing?" demanded Luke.

"Polishing my shoes," Resus said matter-of-factly.

"Here?"

"Why not?" Resus shrugged. "There's nothing wrong with looking your best."

"We're in the middle of nowhere!" exclaimed Luke. "Who exactly are you planning to look your best *for*?"

"Well, Count Negatov is my ancestor," said Resus. "I want to look good for him when we finally reach his castle."

"And we'll never get there if you stop to clean yourself up every ten minutes," Luke remarked, walking on.

Grumbling, Resus slid the cleaning kit back into his cape and followed, wiping his shoe on a clump of weeds. Cleo took up the rear, her eyes darting around at every tiny noise.

The trio continued in silence for almost an hour. As midday approached, the sun, mostly

hidden above a ceiling of churning gray clouds,
cast a thin, watery glow over the landscape.

Eventually, Resus broke the silence. "What sort
of animals do you think there are around here?"

"I can't imagine much wildlife surviving in a
place like this," said Luke. "Why?"

"That stuff on my shoe is starting to smell."

"Will you stop whining about your shoe!"
pleaded Luke. "It's only mud."

"That's the thing," said Resus. "I don't think
it *is* mud. . . ." He held up his foot for the others
to examine.

As Luke came closer, an overpowering stench hit him in the face. "That reeks!" he cried, covering his nose.

"It's not doing the leather any good, either," said Resus.

"How can it be animal dung?" asked Cleo.

Luke scoured the ground and found another puddle similar to the one Resus had stepped in. "I don't know," he said. "But if it is, it must have been left behind by something big."

"But we haven't seen any sign of life since we left Scream Street," Resus pointed out. "Certainly

nothing big enough to leave that much poop in its wake!"

"Whatever it is, it's long gone," said Luke. "Let's rest here for a while."

"Can I clean my shoes now?" asked Resus hopefully.

Luke grinned. "Yes, if it will shut you up! Just make sure you don't sit in any of that stuff. I doubt there's a washing machine within five hundred miles of here."

"Don't worry," said Resus. "I won't be going near any more —"

"Shh!" It was Cleo. "I heard it again!"

"What?" asked Luke. "The honking?"

"It's more of a growl mixed with a honk."

"You heard a *gronk*?" Resus demanded.

Cleo ignored him and pointed to another clump of greenery. "There's that bush again!" Resus opened his mouth to say something, but shut it again as Luke threw him a warning look.

"That's not the same bush, Cleo," said Luke kindly.

"It looks the same," the mummy insisted. "The leaves ruffle in exactly the same way when the wind blows."

"There are dozens of bushes just like it all over the place," Luke assured her. "I think you're just a bit tired and nervous."

"Don't you patronize me, Luke Watson!" Cleo shouted. "There's *something* else around here—and judging by the size of the droppings Resus keeps stepping in, it's something big!"

"There's nothing here!" said Luke, sweeping his hand across the desolate view. "Whatever it was clearly did its business and left."

Cleo looked out across the moor, squinting in the weak light to try to spot something to prove Luke wrong—but apart from the scattered bushes, there was absolutely nothing in sight. "I'm sorry," she sighed, slumping to the ground. "Maybe I *am* just a bit tired."

Luke sat down on the heather beside her. "Don't worry about it," he said, smiling. "I'm pretty exhausted myself."

Resus groaned as he wiped his shoe. "It's all over my sock too!"

Luke pulled the crystal ball from his pocket and stared into the swirling mists. "How are you doing, Mom?" he asked quietly.

The fog inside the ball began to shape itself

 41

into an image. There was Scream Street—and there was his house! The picture zoomed in toward one of the windows, and Luke was just starting to make out a figure standing in the living room when something reached over his shoulder and snatched the crystal ball from his hand.

Chapter Five
The Birds

Luke looked around in surprise and found himself staring into a pair of large, pale eyes. A huge bird—something like a cross between an emu and a swan—stood beside him, the crystal globe wedged in its pointed beak. Its dark-green feathers ruffled in the breeze as it studied Luke for a moment, then . . .

Honk!

Before anyone could move, the bird turned and ran, its long yellow legs pumping hard, feet pounding on the coarse grass. Immediately, four more fluffy green "bushes" ran after it.

Honk! Honk!

Luke jumped to his feet and gave chase, Resus and Cleo just behind him. The strange-looking birds, however, were far too quick for them, and it wasn't long before the trio was forced to stop, out of breath. The three were simply no match for the birds, with their long legs and tough feet.

"I told you those bushes were following us!" wheezed Cleo.

"What *are* they?" asked Luke, resting his hands on his knees and trying to catch his breath.

"No idea," admitted Resus through big gulps of air. "But I bet they win all the medals at their school's track meets!"

"I think we've said good-bye to that crystal ball," said Cleo.

"But I need it to check on my mom," declared Luke. "We *have* to get it back!"

Resus clutched at the stitch in his side. "Better

get moving, then," he said, panting. "I'll be the one walking slowly behind you."

"We'll never catch them," said Cleo.

"Maybe we don't need to," said Luke. "Look—they've stopped!"

As the three friends watched, the birds checked that they were no longer being followed. Then, as one, they tucked their long necks beneath their wings, folded their legs, and sat down. They now looked exactly like small bushes dotted among the scrub, and if Luke, Resus, and Cleo hadn't seen it with their own eyes, they would have walked right past. It was the perfect camouflage.

"Come on," whispered Luke. Slowly he, Resus, and Cleo crept toward the motionless birds, the soft ground dulling the sound of their footsteps. They stole closer and closer, and before long, Luke could see the glint of the crystal ball sticking out of one of the mounds of feathers.

"Now!" he yelled, diving for it. Instantly, all five birds rose up from the ground and dashed away, honking in terror. Luke crashed down with an "Oof!" and a splat.

Cleo hurried over to help him up, then gagged

as the stench hit her. Luke's shirt was covered in reeking dung. "This is just great," he moaned.

Up ahead, the birds continued to run for a few more yards, then dropped to the ground and hid themselves once again.

Cleo pulled up the bandages on her face to cover her nose, then tore another strip from her arm and used it to wipe off the worst from Luke's shirt. "At least we now know where this came from."

"I wouldn't be so sure," said Resus. "I don't think those bird things, as big as they are, would leave behind droppings that size. Not unless they were seriously ill!"

"Never mind that," said Luke impatiently. "We still have to find a way to get the crystal ball back."

"We could try creeping up on them again," suggested Cleo.

"And it might help if you don't scream 'Now!' before you dive headfirst into the nearest pile of dung," added Resus.

Luke shook his head. "We'll just end up chasing them for miles. They're much faster than us."

"Well, I can't think of another solution," said Resus.

"What about the stuff you've got in your cape for Vampire New Year?"

Resus's eyes began to sparkle. "Brilliant!" he exclaimed. "I could shoot fireworks at the birds, then after they've been ripped apart by—"

"Don't you dare finish that sentence," snapped Cleo.

"It was Luke's idea!" Resus protested.

"Actually, I was thinking more of using the cakes to lure them over to us," Luke admitted.

"No way!" cried Resus. "If my mom ever found out I'd wasted her cakes on some ugly old birds, I'd be sent to my coffin without any TV for a year."

"Then I'll just have to find a way to match

47

their speed," sighed Luke. He took a deep breath and closed his eyes.

Cleo grabbed his arm. "What are you doing?"

Luke opened his eyes again. "I'm going to transform my legs and chase the bird that's got the crystal ball."

"You can't!" she exclaimed.

"Why not?"

"We're outside Scream Street, remember?" said Cleo. "We can't be sure you'll have only a partial transformation. What happens if you turn into a complete werewolf?"

"It should be OK," replied Luke. "We're still on G.H.O.U.L. territory, after all."

"That might be true," said Resus, "but if it doesn't work out, I can't see anywhere around here to hide from an angry wolf!"

"Then I'm out of ideas," admitted Luke. "How can we catch those . . . *things*? Whatever they are."

"It is possible that I could be of assistance," said a muffled voice from the direction of Luke's back pocket.

Luke reached into the pocket and pulled out a book with a golden cover. On the spine was

the title, *The G.H.O.U.L. Guide,* and from the front protruded the face of its author, Samuel Skipstone.

Skipstone opened his eyes, and Resus and Cleo came over to join Luke. "This book contains information about every community in the world that is owned by the Government Housing Of Unusual Life-forms," explained the author. "Just show me what you'd like to know about and I'll find the relevant entry."

"OK," said Luke, turning the book so that Skipstone now faced the large green birds still disguised as bushes among the scrub. "What *are* they?"

Samuel Skipstone stared at them for a moment, then *The G.H.O.U.L. Guide* opened, and he began to flick through the pages. "Here you are," he said, stopping at a page with a drawing of a bird on it. It was identical to the ones they could see in front of them. "These creatures are called nasterns."

"Nasties?" asked Luke.

"No, nasterns," Skipstone corrected him. "They are an ancient species of bird, distantly related to the swan, the ostrich, and the magpie."

49

"*Very* distantly related if you ask me," said Resus. "Like my toothless uncle Boslo, who licks the dessert plates clean every Christmas."

"Vampires from this region used to breed them for food when blood supplies were hard to come by," continued Skipstone.

Cleo screwed up her face. "They *ate* them?" she exclaimed in horror.

Luke studied the drawing of the nastern. "I wonder what they taste like."

"I bet no one knows," said Resus. "I can't imagine anyone would be able to catch one to find out!"

"Actually, they do not always run," said Samuel Skipstone. "Due to their relationship to the magpie, they like shiny objects—which can be used to put them in a trance."

"What kind of trance?" asked Cleo.

"Almost as though they have been hypnotized," explained the author. "They stay rooted to the spot until the chance arises to grab whatever it is they have their eyes on."

"If they like shiny things, that'll be why they followed us," said Resus. "They must have spotted Luke using the crystal ball almost as soon as we stepped through the Hex Hatch."

"So, if we can show them something *else* that's shiny, we might be able to get close enough to get it back," suggested Luke.

Resus began to search through his cloak. "I've got a crowbar, a flashlight, and a drum kit," he said. "None of them very shiny, however."

"Um, I hate to say it, but I don't think we'll need anything else to grab their attention," said Cleo.

"It's true." Resus grinned. "They seem to have taken a *shine* to Mr. Skipstone!"

Luke turned to discover all five nasterns now standing staring fixedly at *The G.H.O.U.L. Guide*. One of the birds had the crystal ball wedged in its beak.

"Of course!" said Luke. "The light is glinting

off the book's cover." He angled *The G.H.O.U.L. Guide* toward the birds. They remained frozen in position, continuing to stare at the book and honking quietly. "OK," he said, taking a cautious step forward. "If we're careful, we can keep them focused on this until we're near enough to snatch the crystal ball."

"Please ensure that you keep me at a safe distance," squeaked Skipstone, his golden eyes wide with terror as Luke carried him closer and closer to the birds. "Nasterns are known for their very sharp beaks!"

Cleo and Resus fell into step beside Luke, and the three of them slowly approached the mesmerized creatures. "You keep Mr. Skipstone safe," whispered the mummy. "I'll grab the crystal ball the first chance I get."

"What can I do?" asked Resus.

"Have your fangs at the ready in case one of them decides to bite!"

The children crept steadily toward the nasterns. Luke could now see the shining cover of *The G.H.O.U.L. Guide* reflected in their hungry eyes.

Cleo flexed her fingers, preparing to lunge for the crystal ball as soon as she was close enough.

Resus licked the tips of his fangs and looked watchfully around him.

And that's when the ground collapsed beneath them, plunging the trio into a deep pit below.

Chapter Six
The Hunters

Luke blinked. Stars flashed before his eyes. He'd hit his head on a rock at the bottom of the pit and could already feel a lump beginning to swell up.

"Is everyone OK?" he asked, rubbing his head.

"I'm fine," said Cleo. "I landed on something soft."

"That was me," groaned Resus. "Feel free to get off anytime you want!"

"Mr. Skipstone?" said Luke.

The author opened his eyes. "I seem to have survived the fall unscathed," he assured them.

"Yeah, because *you* landed on me, too," muttered Resus.

Luke clambered to his feet and tucked *The G.H.O.U.L. Guide* back into his pocket. He gazed up at the circle of light above them. The pit was about twenty feet deep and just wide enough for the three children to stand side by side in.

"Where are we?" Cleo asked.

"Some sort of hole, by the looks of it," replied Luke.

"Oh, well done, Detective Inspector Watson," said Resus sarcastically. "However did you work that one out?"

"Cleo should have landed on you a bit harder," Luke said, scowling. "What I was *about* to say is that the hole isn't natural." He ran his fingers along thick grooves in the hard earth. "Someone has dug this out deliberately and covered it with sticks and moss so it wouldn't be seen."

"You mean it's man-made?" said Cleo.

"Not exactly *man*-made," growled a deep voice above them.

The trio looked up to see two huge faces glaring down into the hole.

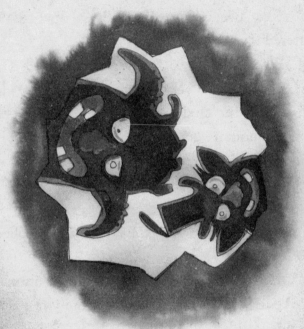

"Trolls!" cried Cleo.

"That one's quite intelligent," rumbled the smaller of the two. "I think we'll save *her* for dessert."

"You try to eat her, and she'll give you indigestion!" shouted Resus.

"And *he's* gonna be the appetizer," grunted the troll.

"You monsters!" yelled Cleo.

The smaller troll almost looked offended. "Comments like that hurt," he said, pouting. "We're not monsters! I'm Stumper, and this is Little Bennett."

"Hello!" called the bigger one cheerily.

"If he's *Little* Bennett," said Luke quietly, "I don't want to run into his big brother anytime soon."

"I appreciate that you might be unwilling to form a lasting friendship," Stumper called down. "What with us having trapped you in order to eat the flesh from your bones. But I'm sure that once you get to know us, you'll agree we're anything but monsters. Get them out of there, Bennett!"

The larger troll grinned, revealing a row of thick teeth that resembled chipped gravestones. "Yes, boss," he said, saluting so hard that he slapped himself in the face. *"Ow!"*

Stumper shook his head. "Just lower the rope!"

Little Bennett began to feed a thick rope down into the pit.

"Do you really think we're going to climb

 57

up that just so you can eat us alive?" demanded Luke.

Stumper shrugged. "You can stay down there and starve to death if you like," he snarled. "Then we'll just drag you up and eat you dead. Makes no difference."

"Maybe we'll tunnel our way out," Cleo called up bravely.

The small troll gave a horrible laugh. "You can try," he mocked. "But I can't see you getting very far unless you've got some of these." He held his thick fist out over the pit and wiggled his fingers. They ended in broad, yellowing claws.

Resus glanced down at his own false fingernails and gulped.

"I think we'll just have to climb up there," Luke said to the others.

"Great idea!" replied Resus. "I tell you what, let's ask them to throw some butter down first. Then we can baste ourselves on the way up!"

"I'm not going to let them eat us," hissed Luke, lowering his voice. "I'll go up first and trigger my transformation once I'm at the top. If everything goes according to plan, I'll face them as a fully formed werewolf."

"Will your werewolf be enough to fight off a pair of trolls?" asked Cleo.

"It's the best chance we've got," replied Luke. He grabbed hold of the rope and started to climb.

Above them, Little Bennett's smile grew wider. A tongue the size of a sofa cushion shot out and licked a pair of leathery lips. "Da first one's coming up da rope, boss!" he bellowed. "Can I eat him as soon as he gets to da top?"

Stumper scowled. "You don't eat them *raw*, bricks-for-brains!" he scolded. "We're not completely uncivilized."

Resus and Cleo watched as Luke came to the top of the rope, and Little Bennett stretched down to pull him out of the hole. "Any second now," whispered the vampire, picturing Luke's face twisting as he transformed into a vicious werewolf. "Just listen for the growls. . . ."

But no growls came. The only noise at all was the rumble of Little Bennett giggling.

Suddenly, the rope dropped back into the hole. "Next!" called Stumper.

Resus and Cleo looked at each other nervously. "It hasn't worked," whispered the mummy. "He hasn't transformed!"

 59

Resus gritted his teeth. "We'll have to go up to see what's going on."

Cleo nodded, then wrapping her fingers around the rope, and began to climb. As she neared the opening of the pit, she, too, was dragged out by Little Bennett. Resus swallowed hard and climbed up after her.

Resus felt himself being pulled out into the daylight by the huge troll, and he looked up to see his friends tied together a few yards away. A long, furry tail wagged from the back of Luke's jeans.

"So I guess you only managed a partial transformation," Resus said with a sigh.

"It's not my fault," insisted Luke. "I tried!"

While Resus was being bound, Luke examined the pair of trolls, hoping to spot something that would help the trio to escape. Stumper, despite being the smaller of the two, was still a good three feet taller than an adult human. His dark-gray skin was covered in scraps of cloth, and he wore a necklace made from shiny silverware, shards of glass, and pieces of tinfoil. His hair was as gray as his skin and slicked back with some sort of wet slime. Perched on top was a battered old top hat.

Little Bennett, now busily tying knots around
Resus's legs, was roughly the size of a small hill. His
black hair was matted into thick dreadlocks that
looked as though they had never been washed,
and he wore a belt of skulls around his waist.

Stumper limped over to inspect his captives. The troll was missing one of his legs and had replaced it with the blackened trunk of a dead tree. He swatted at Luke's werewolf's tail with his hand.

"I see we have someone rather interesting among us, Bennett," he sneered.

"Where?" demanded the larger troll, looking around.

"Here!" barked Stumper, grabbing Little Bennett's dreadlocks and forcing his head around to face Luke. "He's a werewolf, you idiot!"

"Ohh!" Realization crossed Little Bennett's face at a snail's pace.

"It's a shame we're so hungry," continued Stumper. "We could have kept you as a pet. Bennett likes his pets."

"They're my special friends," Little Bennett said with a grin, pulling a handful of seeds from the pocket of his filthy pants. The five nasterns immediately leaped up from their hiding places and ran over to peck hungrily at the food.

"So *that's* how they got us to walk over the pit!" said Resus angrily.

"Oh, they're clever birds," replied Stumper, poking Resus in the stomach with a chubby finger. "Feed them right, and they'll do just about anything for you. I might even let them have the fatty bits we leave behind."

Suddenly something caught the smaller troll's eye. "Well, well, well, what do we have here?" Stumper held out his hand and one of the nasterns dropped the crystal ball into his palm. "This is *very* pretty indeed."

Luke struggled against his bonds. "That's mine!" he shouted.

Stumper grinned. "You'll get it back," he said, waving the globe teasingly in Luke's face. "I'll make sure we pop it inside your skull before Little Bennett here ties your head to his belt in the morning." The troll adjusted the angle of his scruffy hat. "Come, Bennett! I have a feeling we're about to be welcomed home."

"Really, boss?"

Chuckling to himself, Stumper limped away toward the distant trees. Little Bennett grabbed the ends of the rope, swung Luke, Resus, and Cleo over his shoulder, and stomped after him.

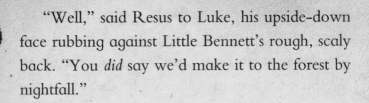

"Well," said Resus to Luke, his upside-down face rubbing against Little Bennett's rough, scaly back. "You *did* say we'd make it to the forest by nightfall."

Chapter Seven
The Village

It took a little under an hour for Stumper and Little Bennett to reach the edge of the wooded area. By this time, Luke, Resus, and Cleo were sore from the rope rubbing on their wrists and ankles and dizzy from swinging side to side as Little Bennett skipped along, chasing after his beloved nasterns.

Eventually a voice brought both trolls to a sudden stop. "Halt! Who's dat wot goes dere?" Luke peered under Little Bennett's armpit and discovered two more trolls blocking their way. These, however, were muscle-bound and armed with sharp spears.

Stumper cleared his throat. "It is I—Pebble J. Stumpington."

"Who?" rumbled the guard.

"*Stumper,* you cretin! I demand to see the Medicine Man at once."

The second guard pointed his spear at the visitors, his brow furrowed in thought. "'Ere, I know you," he grunted. "You're dat bloke wot got frone out of de village for stealin' de Medicine Man's crown!"

Stumper sighed. "I didn't *steal* anything," he said indignantly. "I merely noticed that the crown needed a bit of cleaning. I only wanted to help."

Little Bennett tapped him on the shoulder. "I thought you said you hated the Medicine Man for cutting off your leg and leaving you wiv dat stump."

Stumper gave Little Bennett a swift elbow to the stomach and continued: "I knew that the

Medicine Man wouldn't want to go to the trouble of having the crown spruced up, so I simply took it when he wasn't looking."

"But . . . but . . ." The guard's expression crumpled further as he struggled to compute. "You didn't clean de crown at all. You sold it to some goblins . . ."

"And used de money to buy a dagger," added the first guard.

"Dat you used to stab de Medicine Man in de butt," finished the second.

Little Bennett spoke up again: "Dey're not wrong, boss! You said you'd get de Medicine Man back one day for giving you dat wooden leg."

"Quiet, you fool!" hissed Stumper. "Don't forget, you were banished from the village, too."

"Was I?" inquired Bennett. "Why?"

"*You* knocked out the Medicine Man in the first place so I could steal his crown!"

A grin spread across Bennett's face. "Oh, yeah."

Both guards advanced. "So, what makes you fink we're gonna let you two back into de village?"

"Because . . ." Stumper smiled and snapped

his fingers. Little Bennett swung the children off his back and dumped them at the guards' feet. "I've brought dinner!"

Luke, Resus, and Cleo stood huddled together in a rusted old cooking pot, their arms and legs still bound. All around them, trolls danced and sang to the sound of pounding drums. In the background was a circle of crude mud huts that made up their forest village.

More than a hundred creatures of every shape and size imaginable whooped and squealed with joy as Little Bennett piled armfuls of firewood beneath the cauldron. From a large wooden throne, the Medicine Man watched intently, his face obscured behind a hideous mask. Stumper sat at his side, a smug grin on his face.

"All in all," Resus muttered, "this isn't quite the fun-filled adventure it was supposed to be."

"Are you two OK?" hissed Luke.

"No!" whispered Cleo as a female troll approached and emptied yet another bucket into the filthy liquid already slopping around their knees. "This water's disgusting!"

"Why don't you tell them you'd prefer to be boiled alive in clean water?" suggested Resus. "I'm sure they could arrange it for you."

Little Bennett finished piling up the firewood and dropped to his knees. He banged two pieces of flint together to make a spark.

Cleo leaned over to watch. "That wood will never light," she observed. "It's too wet. He'll need some dry kindling to get the fire—"

"Don't give him *tips*!" roared Resus as Little Bennett smiled toothily and lumbered off.

"We need to think of a way to get out of here—and fast," said Luke.

"And I was just beginning to enjoy myself!" retorted Resus.

"What if we—?"

"SILENCE!"

The drums ceased and the tribe froze as the Medicine Man stood to address them. As the villagers looked on, he slowly removed his repulsive mask—to reveal an identical face underneath.

"Someone fell out of the ugly tree," said Resus.

"And hit every branch on the way down, by the looks of it," added Luke.

The Medicine Man began to speak, shouting out the important words. "You might REMEMBER young STUMPER here visiting me LAST SUMMER, complaining of a BOIL on his TOE." The tribe all scratched their heads and frowned as they tried to access the less-used areas of their brains. "He knew that with my AWESOME POWER I would be able to HEAL his AGONY!"

The trolls cheered and screeched enthusiastically. The Medicine Man stood proudly, accepting the adulation. Then he continued.

"You might also REMEMBER that Stumper did not APPROVE of my SOLUTION to his problem. IN HIS IGNORANCE, he thought that cutting off his WHOLE LEG was too severe a TREATMENT!"

Stumper winced at the memory but quickly replaced it with a smile.

"Banished for his RETALIATORY ACTIONS, he has now RETURNED to us," bellowed the Medicine Man. "Returned to us with the GIFT of FOOD!"

Luke, Resus, and Cleo shuddered as the trolls all turned in their direction.

"NO LONGER shall we be forced to eat HEATHER and NASTERN DUNG!" the Medicine Man exclaimed. "TONIGHT we dine on HUMAN FLESH!"

Once again, the entire tribe went crazy, singing, dancing, and beating drums.

"But BEFORE WE EAT . . ."

The tribe, impatient at the further delay, struggled to quiet down and listen to their leader.

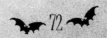 72

One voice could be heard to mutter quietly, "Get on with it!"

"Before we eat," repeated the Medicine Man, "I shall DEMONSTRATE for you my INCREDIBLE MAGICAL POWERS!" Turning toward Stumper, he produced several strips of tree bark from behind his throne.

"PICK A CARD, ANY CARD!"

As Stumper reluctantly took one of the cards, Little Bennett returned with an armful of dry reeds. He packed the grass over the wood beneath the cauldron and once again struck his flints together. The pile lit instantly.

"He's got it going," Cleo commented.

"Yeah," said Resus, "but only because you told him how fire works."

"That's it!" exclaimed Luke. "Fireworks!"

"What?" asked Cleo.

"The fireworks in Resus's cloak!" replied Luke excitedly. "If we can dump them all on the fire, the explosions might freak out the trolls and give us a chance to escape."

"Brilliant!" said Resus, grinning. "But how do we get them out of my cape? All our hands are tied."

"Leave that to me," said Luke. "Seeing as I'm in the swing of partial transformations, we might just live to tell the *tail*. . . ." He closed his eyes and concentrated on sending feelings of anger toward the base of his spine. Within seconds a long, bushy werewolf's tail began to sprout over the top of his jeans.

"Quick as you can," urged Cleo. "My feet are starting to feel warm!"

"And I don't know how much longer these guys are going to wait before jumping in and eating us raw," added Resus. Several of the creatures were already watching them with hungry eyes.

Meanwhile, around the clearing, other trolls stifled yawns as the Medicine Man moved from card tricks to producing a nastern's egg from behind Stumper's ear. "And NOW I want you to think of a NUMBER between ONE and THREE. . . ."

"OK, I'm ready," hissed Luke.

Resus wriggled himself around, allowing Luke to slip his long tail under the edge of his cloak. "The fireworks should be somewhere near the top," whispered the vampire. "Just above the picnic table. Careful—that tickles!"

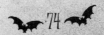

74

"Now, if I reach inside the MAGIC BAG . . . ," announced the Medicine Man.

Luke found the bundle of rockets and sparklers and wrapped his tail around them. Then, in one swift motion, he pulled them out of Resus's cloak and dumped them over the side of the cooking pot, into the fire.

Little Bennett was on his hands and knees, blowing gently on the flames, when the village exploded.

Chapter Eight
The Night

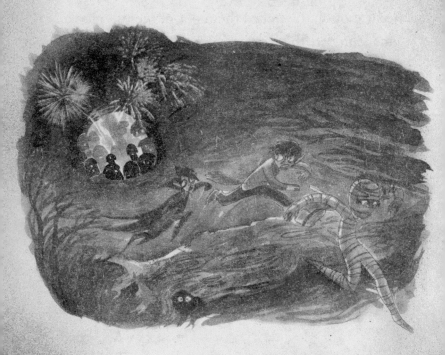

"How much of a head start do you think we've got?" asked Cleo as she, Luke, and Resus raced through the forest.

"Ten minutes at the most, I'd imagine," replied Luke. "I just hope we're heading in the right direction. All I can see are purple and green swirls!"

The fireworks had erupted spectacularly, sending colorful explosions and screaming rockets shooting through the village. As Luke had hoped, the trolls had been terrified—all except for the Medicine Man, who had stared down at his hands in amazement, wondering if he had just come up with his finest magic yet.

As soon as the fireworks display had begun, the trio had flung themselves to one side of the cauldron, which tipped over and crashed to the ground. Pausing only to burn through their bonds, they'd run blindly into the dense forest without a backward glance.

"I just wish we'd had time to get the crystal ball," said Resus. "I stuck my hand into Little Bennett's pocket before we ran, but all I got was a handful of birdseed."

"You put your hand in his pocket to get the crystal ball?" asked Cleo. "Shame it had already been taken!" And she produced the globe from the bandages around her waist.

Luke took it from her with a grin. "You wily little thief!"

Cleo gave a curtsy. "I'm not just a pretty face, you know."

Suddenly, a roar echoed through the woods. "Me finks dey went dis way!"

"So much for ten minutes' head start," hissed Resus.

The trio continued to run, the forest growing darker as the sun began to set. The deeper into the woods they raced, the closer the trees stood together. Roots protruded from the ground, causing Luke and Cleo to trip again and again. Low branches whipped Resus across the face. Behind them, they could hear crashes in the undergrowth as the trolls gave chase.

"We need to get off this path," said Luke, peering around into the darkness. "They'll catch us in no time if we don't."

"What path?" demanded Resus as he plunged his foot into yet more troll poop. "Besides — they're trolls. They'll sniff us out whichever way we go."

"Then maybe we can disguise our scent," proposed Luke.

"How can we disguise our . . . ?" Resus's face fell as he realized. "No way!"

Luke reached down and grabbed a handful of the troll dung. "Fine," he said, beginning to smear it over his arms. "You can smell like dinner

if you like. I'm going to get them off my back!"
With a wry face, Cleo began to copy him.

"All right," sighed Resus. "But you owe me a
new shirt."

Two minutes later, Luke, Resus, and Cleo
were all coated in troll dung. The stench was
almost unbearable.

Branches cracked as the trolls drew nearer.
Luke pulled the others behind a clump of bushes
with him, and they waited in silence.

"Come out, you scrawny little humans!" bellowed Stumper, appearing out of the darkness
with Little Bennett in tow. "You might be able
to get one over on those other morons, but you
can't escape from me!"

"Dey aren't answerin', boss," said Little
Bennett. "I don't fink dey can hear you."

"My one chance of getting back into the village and teaching that pathetic Medicine Man
a lesson, and it's ruined by some stupid kids!"
spat Stumper. "I thought you said you had their
scent," he added, turning on his companion.

Luke held his breath as Little Bennett sniffed at
the air. "I did—but now I've lost it," he admitted.
"And I can't smell dat much right now!" The

larger troll, his face bruised and blistered, had two burned-out fireworks wedged up his nostrils.

Stumper pulled them out angrily. "*Now* what can you smell?"

Little Bennett breathed deeply. "I can smell *us.*"

Stumper sneered. "They must be farther ahead than I thought," he growled. "Come on!" The trolls crashed on through the forest, and soon everything was quiet once more.

Luke crept out of the bush and stretched his legs. The others followed. "Now we just need to figure out which direction the castle is in," he said.

"Maybe Mr. Skipstone will know," suggested Cleo.

Wiping his hands on his trousers, Luke pulled *The G.H.O.U.L. Guide* from his pocket. Samuel Skipstone opened his golden eyes and gazed up at the trio in shock. "Goodness me!" he exclaimed. "What on earth happened to you three?"

"It was Luke's idea," said Cleo, pulling the mucky bandages away from her mouth. "He got some of the stuff on him earlier and decided we should all have a turn."

"I kept the trolls from finding us, didn't I?" Luke pointed out. Without waiting for an answer, he turned back to the author. "We're lost, Mr. Skipstone."

Samuel Skipstone stared up at the trees. The light was fading by the second. "Count Negatov's castle is to the west," he said. "Can you remember in which direction the sun set?"

Luke looked at the few patches of sky visible through the treetops. Colorful swirls still danced before his eyes. "No," he admitted.

"Then unless you want to blunder through the forest in the dark, I suggest you camp for the night here and watch for the sunrise in the morning," advised Skipstone. "The castle will be in the opposite direction."

With a sigh, Resus found himself a patch of moss and lay down, his cloak wrapped around him like a blanket. "Great way to spend Vampire New Year," he muttered.

Luke propped himself up against the base of a tree and took out the crystal ball. As he peered into it, he concentrated on Scream Street and watched as tiny houses began to form out of the mists.

Cleo sat down beside him. "Looking in on your mom?" she asked.

Luke nodded. "Funny," he said. "It used to be my dad I worried about most, but since my mom started transforming . . ." His words trailed off.

"She'll get used to being a werewolf," Cleo assured him. "You did." The image inside the globe zoomed over the central square and down a side street.

"It's not that," said Luke. "I know she'll be OK with transforming occasionally. I'm more concerned that she'll hurt someone. With so many normals walking around Scream Street, it's just not safe. I don't think she could live with that."

As the picture in the crystal ball finally settled on 13 Scream Street, Luke could see through the window and into the living room. Both his parents were there, reading—his mom's arm now back to normal.

"'Night," he whispered, and settled down to sleep.

Luke was woken at dawn by the sound of someone screaming. He leaped to his feet, convinced that the trolls must have found them. It turned out to be Resus having a nightmare.

"Wake up!" he ordered, shaking the vampire by the shoulder.

Resus opened his eyes blearily. "I just had the weirdest dream!" he exclaimed, sitting up. "The trolls followed us back to Scream Street and covered everything with poop. We couldn't get rid of the stuff—it was everywhere!" He looked around him in terror. "They're not back again, are they?"

"Well," said Cleo, yawning, "I think we'll be lucky if they didn't hear you shrieking like a banshee in a blender."

"I was *not* shrieking," countered Resus. "It was a manly cry of terror."

"Come off it," said Cleo. "You sounded like a bat with a helium balloon!"

Resus stood and stretched. "Any idea which way we need to go?"

Luke looked around thoughtfully. The clouds had parted a fraction, and he could just make out the red glow of the sunrise. He turned his back on it and pointed through the trees. "This way," he said. "Count Negatov, here we come!"

Chapter Nine
The Castle

Luke, Resus, and Cleo finally emerged from the forest at the foot of a steep hill. At the top stood a black, misshapen castle. Bats circled around a high tower, and the occasional bolt of lightning forked down, reflecting off the windows.

"Oh, come on," said Luke. "That's such a vampire stereotype. All it needs is a howling wolf and it'll be like a cartoon!"

Somewhere in the distance, a wolf howled.

Resus grinned at him and brought some fruit out of his cloak. He shared it among his friends. Once they'd eaten, the trio began to climb the hill, looking nervously over their shoulders every now and then in case the trolls emerged from the forest below.

"Tell me we won't have to go through this each time in order to return all six relics," moaned Resus.

"We might if we want the doorway closed and the normals gone from Scream Street," said Luke, gripping a handful of brush as he pulled himself over a pile of rocks.

"We're still not one hundred percent certain that returning the relics will close the doorway," Cleo reminded them.

"Oh, great," said Resus. "So we might have been almost boiled alive, covered ourselves in poop, and climbed a mountain, all for nothing!"

Eventually they arrived on a flat plain, at the

center of which stood Castle Negatov. It loomed above them, even more imposing than it had looked from below. A huge, rusted portcullis marked the entrance to the fortress, and a moat ran lazily around its base.

"Water!" exclaimed Cleo. "I can finally wash off this horrible stuff!" She ran toward it as fast as she could.

Suddenly a muffled voice cried out, "Luke! Stop her!"

Luke pulled *The G.H.O.U.L. Guide* from his pocket to find Samuel Skipstone looking agitated. "The moat around the castle is filled with piranhas!" warned the author.

Resus and Luke exchanged a glance, then quickly set off after their friend. "Cleo!" they yelled. "Stop!"

"So you can get there first?" called Cleo over her shoulder, picking up the pace. "No way!"

"You don't understand!" bellowed Luke. "There are piran—"

There was a loud splash as Cleo dived head-first into the moat.

Luke and Resus skidded to a halt at the

water's edge. Cleo was swimming around below them, wiping muck from her bandages. "What are you both shouting about?"

"Cleo, get out of the water!" ordered Luke. "Now!"

"There are piranhas in there!" added Resus.

"What?" Cleo exclaimed disbelievingly. "Are you teasing me?"

She gasped as something nipped at her leg. She felt another bite, this time on her hand. Then another, and another . . .

Within seconds, the water around Cleo was churning as thousands of piranhas closed in on her. The mummy screamed and disappeared beneath the frothing surface.

Luke began to pull off his sweatshirt.

"What are you doing?" demanded Resus.

"Someone's got to save her!" insisted Luke.

"If you jump in there, it won't be a rescue attempt—it'll be suicide!"

"Got any better ideas?"

Resus began to rummage around inside his cape. "I must have a rope here somewhere!" he cried. "We can use it to pull Cleo out." He produced object after object, none of which was any

use whatsoever: an anchor, a bottle of no-tears shampoo, a rotting human arm . . .

"Perfect!" exclaimed Luke. He snatched the arm from Resus and hurled it into the moat near where Cleo had disappeared.

"What did you do that for?" demanded Resus. "That belonged to my aunt Lidbury!"

"Then what's it doing in your cape?"

"She said I could have it after she died," replied Resus.

"Then she doesn't need it anymore, does

she?" said Luke. He watched as, one by one, the piranhas followed the scent of the decomposing limb and attacked it hungrily. Cleo floated to the surface, facedown. "Come on!"

The two boys lowered themselves quickly but cautiously into the moat, trying to disturb the water as little as possible. They swam over to Cleo and lifted her head out of the water, kicking their legs gently beneath the surface to carry them to the other side.

"What do we do if the piranha start biting us?" asked Resus nervously.

Luke grinned. "Try biting back!"

When they reached the far bank, Luke climbed out first and grabbed Cleo's arms, pulling her up as Resus pushed from below. The mummy groaned as Luke laid her on the grass. "What happened?" she asked.

"You almost became fish food," said Luke, helping Resus out of the water. "We had to dive in and save you!"

"Even my aunt Lidbury had to lend a hand," quipped the vampire, wringing water out of his cape.

Cleo climbed unsteadily to her feet. "Are you OK?" Luke asked.

"It stings a bit," said Cleo, "but I'll be all right." Her bandages were torn, but she seemed relatively unscathed.

Resus looked up at the large iron portcullis over the entrance to the castle. "OK," he said, "how do we get in?"

"What?" said Luke.

"How do we get inside the castle?" asked Resus.

"I don't know," Luke admitted. "I thought *you* would."

"Me?" demanded Resus. "Why me?"

"Well, you're family."

"What, so you thought I'd have a secret pass-word or something?"

Luke nodded. "Pretty much, yeah."

"Don't be ridiculous," said Resus. "Until I met you, I'd never been outside Scream Street! Now you expect me to have special access to the world's spookiest castle?"

Cleo gripped the rusted bars of the portcullis. "We could try to lift this thing."

"It was made to keep out angry mobs with torches and pitchforks," Resus pointed out. "There's no way three kids will be able to raise it."

"Let's look around the walls, then," suggested Luke. "There could be a back door."

"A back door?" scoffed Resus. "Don't you think a vampire-hating horde might have thought of that? Let's face it—there's just no way through!"

As he finished speaking, a huge boulder sailed over their heads and smashed into the portcullis. The rusted metal exploded, sending sharp pieces of iron flying through the air.

"You were saying?" inquired Cleo as the dust settled.

"I told you I could smell dem again, boss!" a voice shouted.

The trio looked around. Stumper and Little Bennett were on the other side of the moat, leading the Medicine Man and an entire tribe of angry trolls toward the castle. Even the five nasterns were there, honking wildly.

Luke glanced down at his sopping clothes and wished fervently that he was still covered in troll dung.

"You won't get away from me this time," snarled Stumper.

"Quick!" cried Luke. "Into the castle!"

Resus held up his hand. "There's no need to panic," he said. "You're forgetting there's a moat filled with deadly piranhas between us and them."

The trio looked back across the moat, but to their horror, they saw the trolls leaping into the water without a second thought. The piranhas swarmed around them, nipping and biting, but the trolls continued to stride across the moat, swatting the fish away as if they were flies. The trolls' skin was simply too tough to be pierced by the piranhas' sharp teeth.

"OK." Resus gulped. "Now it's time to panic!"

Chapter Ten
The Chase

The trio raced past the shattered portcullis and across a courtyard. On the far side was a large wooden door, and Luke prayed it wouldn't be locked. It wasn't.

They crashed through the door and quickly

slammed it closed behind them, looking back just long enough to see trolls picking up pieces of broken portcullis and gripping them as weapons.

"Barricade!" yelled Luke. He dragged a chair across the floor and wedged it up against the door.

Resus grabbed a suit of armor and threw it across the chair. "It won't hold them back for long."

"It'll give us a minute or two to start looking for the count's coffin," said Luke, panting.

Cleo tore a strip from an ancient tapestry and tied the door handle to a stout metal candleholder set into the wall. "Where do you think it will be?"

"Who knows?" said Luke. "I suppose there could be a crypt underneath us."

Resus shrugged. "If I were Count Negatov, I'd have my coffin placed as high as possible— away from the creepy-crawlies."

The trio looked at one another. "The tower!" they cried together.

Crash!

The door creaked inward a fraction, and the furniture that had been stacked against it moved

back a few inches. "You tricked us!" roared the Medicine Man from the other side of the door. "I don't take that from *any* meal! Now, get out here and be eaten!"

Crash!

This time, one of the sharp lengths of iron made a hole in the door, splintering the wood and sending the suit of armor skittering away across the stone floor.

"This way!" shouted Luke, running toward the middle of the castle, pausing only to pull an ax down from a wall display.

"Do you know how to use one of those?" asked Resus, catching up to him. Cleo was close behind.

"How hard can it be?" replied Luke. "Surely it's just point and chop!"

Unable to argue with this, Resus grabbed a piece of wood with a length of chain attached to it. At the other end of the chain was a spiked metal ball. "I don't know what this is," he said, "but it looks like it could cause a bruise or two!"

"It's called a battle flail," explained Cleo, arming herself with a sword.

"This is no time for a history lesson," said Resus. "Let's go!"

The trio raced along a corridor toward a large stone archway. Behind them, the door finally smashed open. Trolls clambered over the pile of furniture and lumbered toward the children with a roar.

"This way!" urged Luke.

The kids ran through the archway and began to climb a spiral stone staircase that Luke hoped led to the tower they had seen from outside the castle. The steps were covered in dust that rose up in clouds around their heads as they ran.

"I'm getting dizzy," said Resus, coughing. "And it feels like my legs are on fire!"

Behind him, Cleo clutched her sword in both hands, pointing it out in front of her. "Don't slow down, whatever you do," she warned. "Or I won't be responsible for the consequences!"

The trolls reached the bottom of the staircase. There was a smack.

"*Ow!*" grunted Little Bennett, rubbing his head.

"You idiot!" bawled Stumper. "If the arch was too low, why didn't you duck?"

"I didn't know it was!" protested the huge troll. "I can't fit froo dere!"

"Well, it's a good thing *I* can," barked Stumper. "Now get outside and wait at the bottom of the tower. I'll grab those horrible kids at the top and toss them down to you!"

"Do I have to catch dem?"

The smaller troll grinned. "Not if you don't want to."

"WHERE are THEY?" demanded the Medicine Man, skidding to a halt beside Stumper. The rest of the tribe was now packed into the hall, awaiting instructions.

"They went that way," lied Stumper, pointing down a long, unlit corridor.

"TEAR the place APART!" the Medicine Man roared to his troops, and he led the eager trolls deeper into the castle, leaving Stumper alone at the bottom of the tower.

"You're all mine, kiddies," snarled the troll, placing his foot on the bottom step. His wooden leg clicked as he climbed. *Thump, click. Thump, click. Thump, click.*

By now, Luke, Resus, and Cleo had reached a small landing at the top of the tower. Off it

98

stood the entrance to a single room. This door, however, *was* locked.

Resus slipped one of his fake vampire nails into the lock and began to twist.

Thump, click. Thump, click. Thump, click. Stumper was getting closer. "You can't get away from me, little tasties," he called.

"Hurry up!" Cleo urged Resus.

"I'm trying," retorted the vampire, but his hands were shaking too much.

"It'll take too long," barked Luke. "Get back!" As soon as Resus was clear, Luke swung his ax and smashed it into the door. The wood cracked as the blade plunged deep into the grain.

Again and again he struck at the door with the heavy weapon, gradually creating a hole near the lock. The noise of metal striking wood wasn't enough to drown out the approaching footsteps, however, and they were becoming louder.

Thump, click. Thump, click. Thump, click.

Yelling with frustration, Resus swung the mace around his head and struck the door handle as hard as he could with the spiked ball. The lock shattered from the force of the blow, and the door swung open.

Thump, click.

Just as Luke, Resus, and Cleo dashed into the room, Stumper appeared on the landing, a wicked smile playing across his face. "Lunchtime!" he gurgled.

The trio backed farther into the tiny room and found themselves pressed against a shiny black coffin that lay on a table at its center. Stained-glass windows cast brightly colored shapes across the polished casket.

Resus took Count Negatov's fang from his cloak and handed it to Luke. "We should return this," he said. "If it's the last thing we do."

"Don't be ridiculous," snarled Stumper, following them into the room. "The last thing you do will be to taste delicious!"

Resus and Cleo spun around and pushed hard against the lid of the coffin. It wouldn't move.

"We've got to open it," said Luke, coming over to help them. "Count Negatov's body is in there!"

"I think you'll find that it isn't," announced a voice — and Count Negatov stepped out from behind the broken door.

Luke looked at Resus in amazement. "Do you vampires *ever* die?"

Count Negatov raised an eyebrow. "I *was* at peace," he declared calmly, "but the manner in which you opened my door would wake even the dead!"

Stumper drew himself up to his full height before the count. "Out of my way, vampire!" he ordered. "You're standing between me and my next meal."

"Who are you to issue commands to Count Negatov in his own castle?" boomed the count.

"I am Stumper," proclaimed the troll, less confidently this time. "Soon to be Medicine Man of my tribe and master of all the lands you see before you." He pointed vaguely out the window, but his hand was shaking.

"NO!" roared Count Negatov. "You are nothing!" Then he lunged forward, gripped Stumper, and lifted him clear off the ground. Without hesitation, he hurled the troll through the stained-glass window—and then there was silence.

Count Negatov turned back to Luke, Resus, and Cleo. "Do I know you children?"

"I am Resus Negative," said Resus, holding up his hand so the count could examine his palm. "Descendant of the glorious line of Negatov."

"And I'm Luke Watson," added Luke. "You gave me the gift of your fang so I could take my parents away from Scream Street."

Cleo smiled sweetly. "I'm just here to keep these two out of trouble."

"We have come to return the fang," explained Luke.

"Return it?" inquired Negatov. "Why?"

"It's a long story," Resus said with a sigh. "Let's just say his mom and dad saw the benefits of Luke's staying among his own kind."

"Very well," replied the count, holding out his hand.

Luke took a deep breath and handed back the fang.

Nothing happened.

"Well?" asked Cleo excitedly. "Did it work?"

"Hang on," said Luke. He took the crystal ball from his pocket, and the trio crowded around to watch Scream Street appear. In the central square, they could see a tiny image of Sir Otto Sneer sitting on his stool in front of the rainbow-colored doorway.

Resus gave a sigh of disappointment. "It didn't work. We came all this way for nothing!"

Luke stared silently at the crowd of normals exploring Scream Street.

"The fang is not yet completely returned," Count Negatov reminded them. And he opened his mouth and slipped the tooth back into his upper gum.

Suddenly, the red light within the multicolored doorway exploded into a shower of sparks, lighting up the crystal ball in a crimson glow. Sir Otto dived for cover as scarlet flares burst from the arch and shot across the square. Peering more closely,

the trio could see that the doorway remained open, but it appeared to be smaller than before and the red color had vanished.

"It worked!" cried Luke.

"And Resus got his fireworks for Vampire New Year," added Cleo.

"All right!" Resus cried, giving Cleo a high-five. "Now all we need to do is return the other relics and it's bye-bye, normals!"

"We have to get home first," Cleo reminded him. "Starting with a trip back down that staircase."

Resus groaned. "I don't think my legs can take it."

Count Negatov rested his hand on the shoulder of his distant descendant and smiled. "Then let me show you the *real* reason for having my coffin placed up here."

Chapter Eleven
The Gift

Cleo squealed with excitement and the ends of her bandages whipped out behind her. She, Resus, and Luke were sitting on the polished coffin lid, surfing their way down the spiral staircase.

"It's official," Luke said, grinning. "All vampires are crazy!"

"Do you want to go back up there and tell the count that?" asked Resus.

"I doubt there's much chance of us turning this thing around."

When it reached the bottom of the staircase, the coffin lid shot smoothly along the corridor and across the stone floor of the entrance hall, toward the exit. Luke expected them to slow down any moment, but if anything, they seemed to be picking up speed.

"Do you think we could get all the way to the Hex Hatch on this?" said Cleo, giggling and gripping Resus's shoulders.

Luke gritted his teeth when he saw the discarded suit of armor in their path. "We'll be stopping right here unless we all lean to the left!" he shouted. Cleo and Resus did as he said, and the coffin lid swished straight past the armor.

The rest of the entrance hall had been cleared of obstructions by their pursuers, so the trio flew out of the castle door and into the courtyard without another hitch. "Look out!" shouted

107

Luke, struggling to keep his balance as they hit the cobblestones.

Suddenly, Little Bennett and a very bruised Stumper stepped out in front of them.

"Duck!" yelled Resus. The three of them crouched down together and shot between Little Bennett's legs. Stumper growled and spun around, only to receive a crack across his good knee with a studded metal ball.

"WHAT WAS THAT?" he thundered, clutching at his leg in pain.

"A battle flail!" Resus shouted with glee, tucking it into his cape.

Soon the coffin lid was speeding across the grass toward the moat. On the far side, the five nasterns crouched low and watched the trio's swift approach. "We need to jump off!" called Luke.

"No, we don't!" screamed Cleo. "Just keep your nerve!"

When the makeshift surfboard hit the surface of the water, it sent up a wave of spray behind it but continued to glide across the moat at top speed. Then it crashed into the far bank, finally coming to a stop. The trio went sprawling, and the nasterns shrieked and leaped into the air.

"That was *awesome,*" said Cleo, jumping to her feet.

Luke looked back across the moat. Stumper and Little Bennett were already striding through the water, and the rest of the tribe had appeared in the courtyard behind them, led by the enraged Medicine Man. "I think we'd better run," he said.

Resus shook his head. "Not when we've got these guys to help us." He took a handful of seeds from his pocket and held it out. The nasterns scurried over. "Remember what Stumper said? Feed them well and they'll do just about anything."

He grabbed hold of the nearest bird by its neck and swung himself onto its back. "Anyone care to take the quick way home?"

Luke and Cleo didn't hesitate. They jumped onto the backs of two of the other nasterns and, with a click of their heels, sent the birds racing down the side of the hill toward the forest. They clung on tight.

"Get back here!" raged Stumper, emerging from the water and running after them. Despite his wooden leg, the troll was fast when he was going downhill, and before long he had almost caught up to them.

"I'll make you pay for this. I'll eat you all alive!"

Resus grinned over his shoulder. "You said it yourself: it's better to cook us first!" he shouted. "And for that you'll need fire." He plunged his hand into his cloak and pulled out a flaming torch. Leaning backward until he was lying almost flat on the nastern's back, he gripped its neck with one hand and touched the flame to Stumper's wooden leg with the other.

The dry, dead wood of the artificial limb burst

alight almost instantly. It snapped, and with a squeal, the troll tumbled to the ground, landing face-first in a pile of dung.

Resus pulled himself upright and put the torch away. "We'll send the birds back to you, Little Bennett!" he called over his shoulder.

"OK," replied the huge troll, waving at the trio's retreating backs as he stopped to help Stumper back up onto his remaining foot. "See you later!"

"YOU IDIOT!" bellowed Stumper, his muck-covered face turning purple with rage. "You're almost as stupid as that bone-headed, talentless Medicine Man!"

"WHAT did you SAY?" roared a voice. Stumper spun around to find himself surrounded by trolls, the furious Medicine Man at their head.

"I—I, er . . ." Stumper stammered. "I mean . . ."

"Take him BACK to the VILLAGE," the Medicine Man ordered. "I have a new MAGIC TRICK I would like to try out—SAWING A TROLL IN HALF!"

Luke, Resus, and Cleo arrived at the Hex Hatch just as the sun began to set. They climbed down from the nasterns, and Resus treated the birds to the remainder of the seeds from his pocket.

"Do you think they will return to Little Bennett?" asked Cleo.

"Who knows?" said Luke. "Maybe they'll just keep to themselves for a while."

Resus watched them with a smile as they sat down where they were and curled up into their little bush shapes to sleep. "You don't think I'd be able to take one of them home with me, do you?" he asked.

Cleo snorted out a laugh. "Where would you keep a seventy-pound parakeet?"

"Good point." Resus laughed. And with a final look at his ancestor's homeland, he climbed through the Hex Hatch and back into Scream Street. Luke and Cleo followed.

The sky glowed red with the approaching sunset as they wandered toward the central square. "Are you guys going straight home?" Cleo asked.

"What, and miss the fireworks?" Luke smiled.

Cleo looked at him, confused. "Is it still Vampire New Year?" she asked. "I thought that was last night."

"Not *those* fireworks," said Luke, his eyes twinkling. "Follow me."

Sir Otto Sneer spotted the trio as soon as they stepped into the square. He leaped from his stool and waddled toward them angrily. "What did you freaks do to my doorway?" he demanded.

Luke looked over at the shimmering lights that made up the doorway back to the real world. Only five colors remained—blue, yellow, purple, green, and orange—and it was true, the entrance seemed to have shrunk a little. "We didn't do anything," he said sweetly.

Sneer bit down hard on his cigar. "You've done something to one of the relics, haven't you?" he growled. He pointed to Resus's cape and thrust his hand out toward the trio. "Whatever else you've got in there, you'd better give it to me—right now."

"With pleasure," said Resus, sweeping his hand out from under his cloak and slopping a lump of reeking gray troll dung into the landlord's hand.

Sir Otto yelped in disgust and hurled it to the ground, staring at his filthy fingers in horror.

Then he turned and raced away toward Sneer Hall, cursing the children as he went.

"I thought you hated that stuff!" exclaimed Cleo, holding her nose.

"I do," said Resus. "But I figured it would be rude to go all that way and not bring Sneer back a little souvenir."

Luke laughed. "It doesn't look like he was too happy with your choice of gift."

"Well, if he doesn't want the stuff, we can

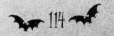

sure make good use of it," said a voice. The trio turned to see Doug and Berry lurching toward them.

Doug eyed the troll dung with glee. "It'll make a terrific mud pack—perfect for Berry's complexion!"

"It's all yours," said Resus. "Unless, of course, Luke wants it."

"No, really!" insisted Luke.

"Why, thank you, children." Berry beamed. She bent to scoop up the dung, and the zombies limped away.

Resus brought the golden casket of relics out of his cloak and opened it up. "OK, then," he said. "What's next?"

"The bottle of witch's blood was the second relic we found," said Luke. "So I guess it should be the next one we give back."

Cleo yawned. "Just tell me you don't want to go now."

"I'm not going anywhere until I've had a bath!" exclaimed Resus.

Luke laughed. "Sounds like a good idea," he said. "But before I do anything else, I'm going home to see my mom."

 115

Tommy Donbavand was born and raised in Liverpool, England, and has held a variety of jobs, including clown, actor, theater producer, children's entertainer, drama teacher, storyteller, and writer. His nonfiction books for children and their parents, *Boredom Busters* and *Quick Fixes for Bored Kids,* have helped him to become a regular guest on radio stations around the U.K. He also writes for a number of magazines, including *Creative Steps* and Scholastic's *Junior Education*.

Tommy sees the Scream Street series as what might have resulted had Stephen King been a writer for *Scooby-Doo*. "Writing the Scream Street books is fangtastic fun," he says. "I just have to be careful not to scare myself too much!" Tommy had so much fun writing the first books that he decided to give Luke, Resus, and Cleo another quest so he'd have an excuse to write some more.